Published by Hachette Partworks Ltd
ISBN: 978-1-906965-43-3
Date of Printing: June 2010
Printed in Singapore by Tien Wah Press

DISNEP · PIXAR

TOY STORY
3

DISNEP · PIXAR

H hachette

Andy was a teenager. He was about to go to college and he didn't want to play with his toys any more.

"Let's get to work here," Andy's mother said. "Anything you're not taking to college either goes in the attic, or it's trash." Then she suggested that he could donate his old toys to the nursery.

"No one's going to want them," he told her. "They're junk."

Inside the toy box, the toys gasped!

Andy put all his toys except Woody into a bag. He had decided to take Woody to college with him.

Woody peeked into the hallway. What a relief! It looked as if Andy had changed his mind – he was heading for the attic with the toys. They wouldn't be thrown away, after all! Suddenly Molly called for help. Andy dropped the bag of toys and went to see what she wanted. Then Andy's mother spotted the bag. She thought it was rubbish, so she picked it up and carried it outside.

Woody was horrified – Andy's mother was making a huge mistake!

Woody raced off to find the other toys and rescue them. Too late! The dustcart arrived and the bags were tossed into the back of the truck.

Then Woody spotted his friends clambering into the car. They were still alive! Jessie had convinced them to climb into the box that Andy's mother was going to donate to Sunnyside Daycare nursery.

"Andy threw us out!" exclaimed Slinky. They all thought it was Andy who had dumped them.

Woody tried to explain that it was a mistake, but the other toys didn't believe him.

SLAM! Andy's mother got into the car and drove off. During the journey, Woody tried to convince the other toys to come back home with him. He told them the nursery would be a sad, lonely place.

But when they arrived, the toys were amazed. Sunnyside looked wonderful to them. And the other toys were friendly! Friendliest of all was a big, pink bear who smelled like strawberries.

"Welcome to Sunnyside!" he said. "Call me Lotso!"

Lotso and a doll named Big Baby led the toys around Sunnyside, before showing them to their new home, the Caterpillar Room.

"Look at this place!" cried Jessie excitedly.

After Lotso left, Andy's toys eagerly waited for the children to arrive. They hadn't been played with in a long time! Everyone was happy with their new home... except Woody, who still wasn't convinced.

"So this is it?" Woody asked his friends. "After all we've been through?"

No one replied, so Woody walked away, all alone.

Woody climbed through a window and onto the roof. He found an old kite and decided to use it to escape. But as he floated over the playground, a sudden gust of wind blew up and broke the kite. Woody hurtled towards the ground but luckily, his pull-string caught in a branch. He was saved!

A little girl called Bonnie ran over to the dangling cowboy. She grabbed Woody and shoved him into her backpack.

Meanwhile, a crowd of toddlers burst into the Caterpillar Room. But playtime didn't turn out as Andy's toys had hoped. The children played with them very roughly! This wasn't fun at all. It was horrible!

One screaming toddler threw Buzz in the air and he landed on the window sill. He peeked through the window into the Butterfly Room. There, a group of four- and five-year-olds were playing gently with Lotso and the other toys. Buzz couldn't believe his eyes!

Later, when the children had all gone home, the toys were left miserable and aching all over. They wished they could be in the Butterfly Room with the older children.

Buzz offered to go to Lotso and ask about moving. He climbed through a window and into a hallway, where three of Lotso's friends were talking. Buzz followed them and watched as they climbed into a snack machine.

Buzz realised that the Butterfly Room toys were having a meeting.

"So what do you guys think of the new recruits?" asked Ken, a friend of Lotso's. "Any keepers?"

"All of them toys are disposable," sneered another toy. "We'll be lucky if they last us a week!"

Buzz was shocked. They had sent Andy's toys to the Caterpillar Room on purpose! He had to warn his friends. But when Buzz turned to go, Big Baby was waiting for him. Poor Buzz was taken prisoner.

Back in the Caterpillar Room, Mrs. Potato Head shouted, "I see Andy!" She was watching Andy back at his house, through the eye she had accidentally left behind! Seeing how upset Andy was, the toys realised that he had never meant to throw them away, after all.

They decided to go home, but Lotso had other ideas.

"You ain't leaving Sunnyside," he snarled.

Just then, Buzz reappeared. His settings had been altered by Lotso, and under Lotso's command, he seized Andy's toys.

Meanwhile, at Bonnie's house, her toys told Woody the truth about Lotso. He had become cruel because he believed his owner had abandoned him. Woody realised that his friends were in danger. He smuggled himself back into Sunnyside in Bonnie's backpack and was horrified when he saw how his friends were being treated!

RIIING! RIIING! A toy telephone sidled up to Woody. The cowboy picked up the receiver and heard, "You and your friends aren't ever getting out of here now." Lotso kept tabs on everyone, the phone said. There was only one way out: the rubbish chute. But first, they would have to steal the keys to the nursery.

Woody rejoined his friends and together they agreed an escape plan.

As night fell, Mr. Potato Head distracted Lotso's gang while Woody and Slinky grabbed the keys. Jessie used the keys to open the door while Rex and Hamm held Buzz down and pressed his 'reset' button.

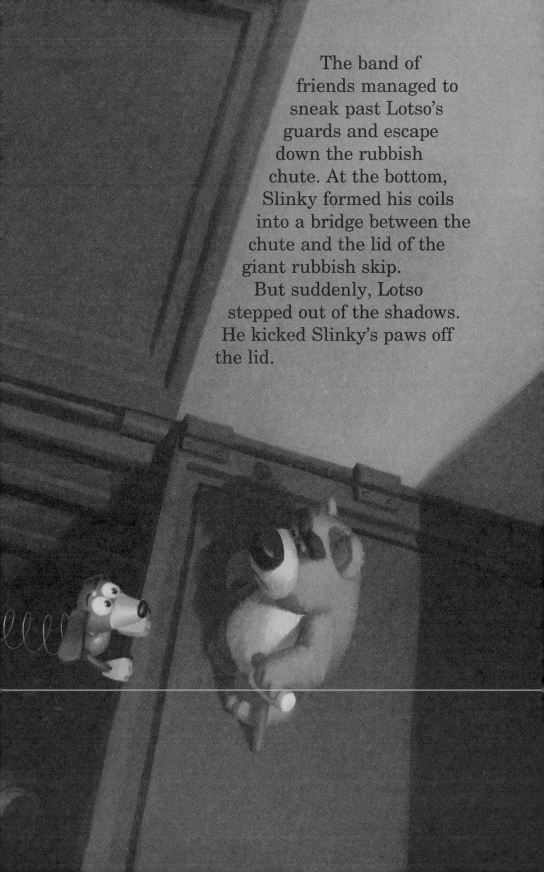

The band of
friends managed to
sneak past Lotso's
guards and escape
down the rubbish
chute. At the bottom,
Slinky formed his coils
into a bridge between the
chute and the lid of the
giant rubbish skip.
But suddenly, Lotso
stepped out of the shadows.
He kicked Slinky's paws off
the lid.

After a struggle, the toys all ended up in the skip. Then the rubbish truck arrived. It lifted the container and everything began to tip out. The poor toys had nothing to hang on to!

"Woody!" Jessie shouted, grabbing for the cowboy's hand.

But Woody and all the other toys, including Lotso, tumbled into the waiting truck.

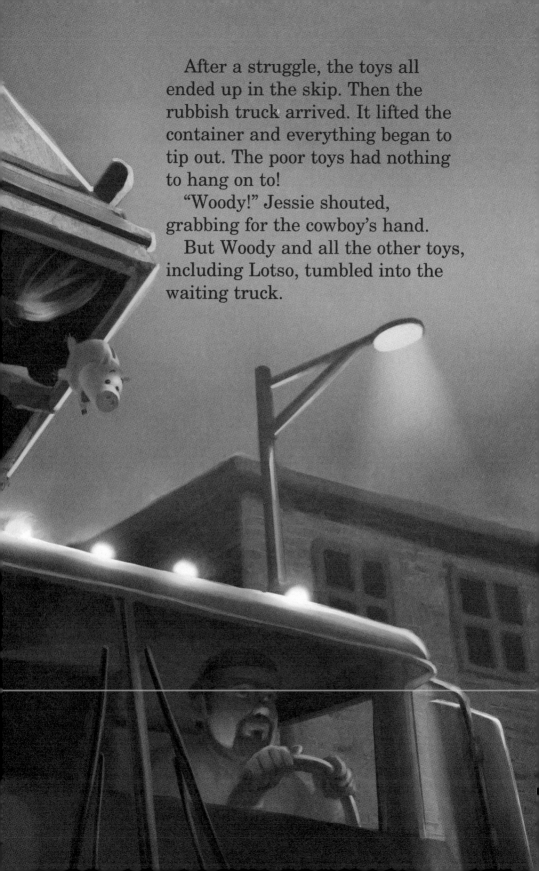

Soon, the rubbish truck arrived at the Tri-County Landfill and dumped its load onto the ground.

While the Aliens ran off towards a huge crane, a bulldozer pushed the rest of the toys onto a conveyor belt.

Suddenly, a furry pink paw reached out from underneath a golf bag. "Help!" begged Lotso.

Woody and Buzz used a golf club to free the trapped bear and lift them up to a magnetic conveyor belt above.

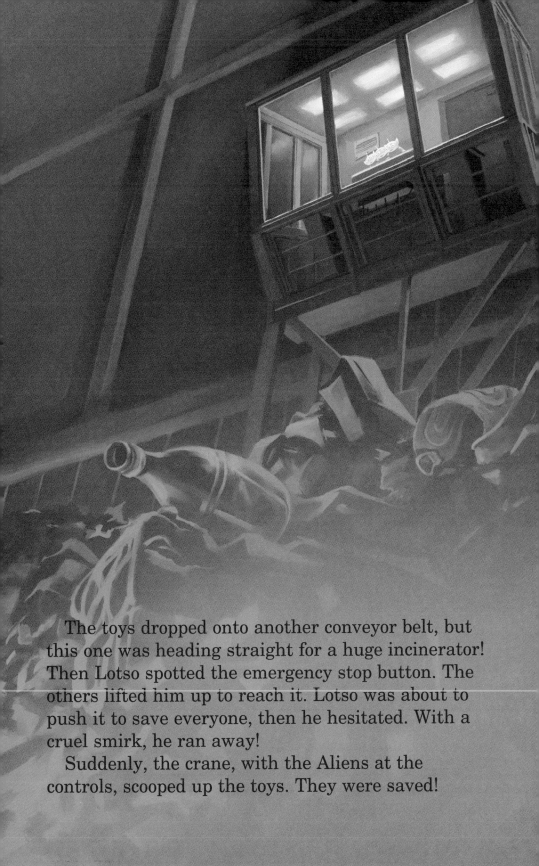

The toys dropped onto another conveyor belt, but this one was heading straight for a huge incinerator! Then Lotso spotted the emergency stop button. The others lifted him up to reach it. Lotso was about to push it to save everyone, then he hesitated. With a cruel smirk, he ran away!

Suddenly, the crane, with the Aliens at the controls, scooped up the toys. They were saved!

But there was no time to celebrate. "Come on, Woody," said Jessie. "We've got to get you home."

"What about you guys?" Woody asked. "Maybe the attic's not such a great idea."

"We'll be there for Andy," Buzz declared.

"Together," Jessie added. "That's what matters."

Then the toys spotted their local rubbish collector climbing into his truck. The toys hurried to hitch a ride home.

Lotso found his way onto a different truck. But he wouldn't be hopping off any time soon!

The toys finally arrived at Andy's house. Buzz helped the toys into the *ATTIC* box, while Woody headed for the box marked *COLLEGE*.

Inside the box, Woody found a photo of Andy surrounded by his toys. It gave him an idea. Woody sneaked across the room and hastily wrote something on a sticky note. Quickly, he stuck the note on the attic box.

When Andy returned to move the last boxes, he saw the sticky note. He opened the box and got a wonderful surprise – there were the toys he thought had been thrown away! Then he looked more closely at the note.

After reading the note, Andy took the box to Bonnie's house.

"Someone told me you're really good with toys," Andy told the little girl. "These are mine, but I'm going away now, so I need someone really special to look after them."

He gave Bonnie the toys, one by one. But when he got to Woody, Andy hesitated. Woody didn't belong there! Then, realising that Bonnie already loved Woody and that she would take good care of him, Andy handed over his favourite cowboy.

In the car, Andy took one last look back at his toys. "Bye, guys," he said quietly before driving off. The toys watched Andy disappear down the street.

"So long, partner," said Woody.

Buzz and the others gathered around him. Their life with Andy was ending, but their adventures with Bonnie had just begun.

ATTIC